WINNIPEG

DEC 2 3 2010

PUBLIC LIBRARY

WITHDRAWN

D1442312

JAN 0 5 2011

Which Way to Witch School?

Scott Santoro

HARPER

An Imprint of HarperCollinsPublishers

Which Way to Witch School?
Copyright © 2010 by Scott Santoro
All rights reserved.
Manufactured in China.
No part of this book may be used or reproduced in any manner whatsoever without written permission
except in the case of brief quotations embodied in critical articles and reviews. For information address
HarperCollins Children's Books, a division of HarperCollins Publishers,
10 East 53rd Street, New York, NY 10022.
www.harpercollinschildrens.com

Library of Congress Cataloging-in-Publication Data is available.
ISBN 978-0-06-078181-1 (trade bdg.) — ISBN 978-0-06-078182-8 (lib. bdg.)

Typography by Jeanne L. Hogle
10 11 12 13 14 LEO 10 9 8 7 6 5 4 3 2 1
❖
First Edition

For my mother,
who encouraged my dream to become an author
by helping me with my first attempt
at a picture book when I was six years old

Within haunted houses all over the land,
Those far away and those close at hand,
You'll find little witches, not wicked or cruel,
Preparing to go to Miss Thornapple's school.

It's more than exciting, they really can't wait;
There won't be a single witch showing up late.
Packing is simple, it's done just like that.
The trick is to get all your things in your hat.

A bus picks them up and they go as a team.
They all love the driver—they think he's a scream.
With a whoosh the bus lifts them straight up in the air;
They say it will take half the night to get there.

They cackle and joke, they're a fun-loving bunch,
And when they are hungry, they have a box lunch.
The bus dives to the earth, has it run out of fuel?
No, they've simply arrived at Miss Thornapple's school.

The girls are delighted to see the locale,
And each discovers a favorite new pal.
They're eager to trade any gossip and potions,
Especially the ones that cause endless commotions.

Miss Thornapple dines with the girls in the hall
On food as delicious as they can recall.
The eyeballs are gooey, like raspberry jelly,
And tentacles tend to be slimy and smelly.

They move into dorms and make them their own.
They straighten the cobwebs and talk on the phone.

They tell scary stories their grandmothers told
And smuggle in kittens from out of the cold.

If they don't pay attention in class, it's apparent
To teachers who tend to be rather transparent.
Miss Zorch is their teacher in chemistry class,
Which for a witch is important to pass.

Mathematics and physics can often apply
In finding out how magic broomsticks can fly.

Singing is fun, they're determined to reach
The highest of notes, they're the best ones to screech.

But Miss Thornapple's school is not merely pragmatic;
Witches are famous for being dramatic.

Their plays might be funny or terribly tragic
But on opening night there is always some magic.

But it's not just the mind that has to be fed,
Says Miss Glonk, their teacher in physical ed.

It's all very well to swim in a pool,
But to swim in a swamp is especially cool.

Sometimes they explore the haunted old forest.
It's creepy enough to delight any tourist.
Hiking at night is not at all frightening.
In fact it's quite dull without thunder and lightning.

Then, like a spell that a witch could have cast,
In a wink and a flash the school year has passed.
Miss Thornapple wipes a tear from her eye
As she bids all the little witches good-bye.

That may be surprising, but don't be judgmental.
Many a witch can be quite sentimental.

And then with a shudder, a sputter, and wheeze,
The bus takes to the air like a ghost on a breeze.
But don't be too sad, it's not really the end.
Next year they will gather all over again.